The Witch of Windspindle Hollow
By: B. Humphrey

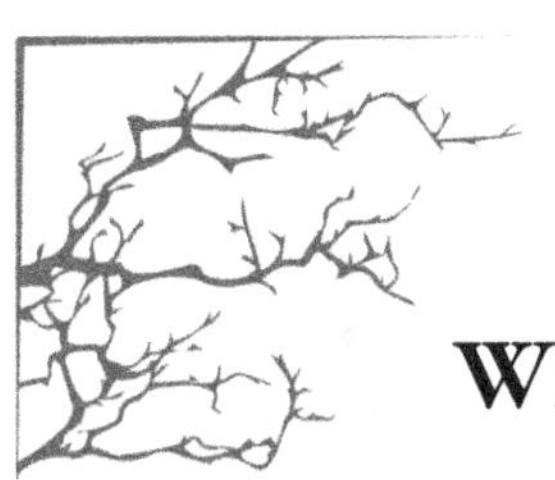

Whispers in the Wind

The day Ivy Brightwater buried her grandmother, the sky broke open in a misty drizzle, as if the clouds had wept with her. She stood under a black umbrella, her hands pale against the fabric of her wool coat, watching the last of the dirt scatter over Liora's simple wooden casket. The wind swirled through the old stone churchyard, carrying whispers through the boughs of yew trees that lined the path. Ivy thought she could almost hear her grandmother's voice—soft, playful, and full of secrets.

"The wind knows, child. If you listen close enough, you'll hear it tell you things no one else can."

That's what Liora used to say whenever they wandered into the woods together, collecting wild herbs and mushrooms for tea. The scent of thyme and lavender still clung to Ivy's memory, even though those carefree afternoons were long gone.

After the funeral, the house felt unbearably quiet. Ivy returned to Liora's cottage on the edge of Greenwick—a little stone house, tucked between overgrown rose bushes and apple trees that leaned lazily toward the sky. It smelled of beeswax, drying herbs, and cinnamon, just as it always had. But the warmth was gone. Ivy wandered from room to room, running her fingers along the spines of books, jars filled with dried petals, and shelves cluttered with trinkets her grandmother had collected over the years.

She found herself in the attic just as the last light of the afternoon slipped through the narrow windows. Dust motes spun lazily in the air, glinting like tiny stars. And there, beneath an old quilt embroidered with oak leaves and moons, Ivy discovered an ancient, worn map with the edges frayed like autumn leaves. Windspindle Hollow was drawn at the center, wrapped in swirling patterns that looked almost like dancing spirits.

Tucked inside the folds of the map was a note. Her grandmother's handwriting, familiar and looping, stretched across the yellowed paper:

"Remember, child—what's lost in the forest is sometimes found again under moonlight."

Ivy held the map tightly, feeling her heart stir in a way it hadn't in months. The name *Windspindle Hollow* tugged at her memory, half-forgotten tales of enchanted woods and strange creatures. Her grandmother had told her bedtime stories of the Hollow—of a forest that breathed like a sleeping giant, where sprites whispered secrets on the wind and mushroom houses glowed under the stars.

But those were just stories, weren't they?

The villagers said otherwise. Windspindle Hollow, they whispered, belonged to a witch. No one dared venture too far into the woods for fear they would be lost forever—claimed by the forest or worse, by the witch who was said to walk among the misty trees.

Ivy traced the lines of the map with her fingertip, following the curling streams and tiny inked symbols that marked glades, caves, and strange places hidden deep in the Hollow. She knew then, with an unshakable certainty, that she had to go there.

Her grandmother had kept this map for a reason. And whatever that reason was, it lay within Windspindle Hollow.

The next morning dawned with pale sunlight spilling across the mist-covered fields, and Ivy slipped quietly from the cottage. She packed a small satchel with essentials—her notebook, a jar of blackberry jam, a thermos of tea, and the map folded neatly into the pocket of her coat. As she stepped out into the crisp autumn air, the scent of woodsmoke drifted from distant chimneys, mingling with the sweet tang of fallen apples.

The villagers eyed her warily as she passed through the cobbled streets of Greenwick. Most of them knew Ivy only as Liora's granddaughter—the girl with wild hair and a restless heart, always with a book under her arm. They offered polite nods but whispered behind her back as she headed toward the forest path.

Windspindle Hollow loomed just beyond the edge of town, wrapped in golden birch trees that swayed gently in the breeze. A low mist curled at the forest's edge, as if the Hollow were breathing, exhaling a sigh of welcome—or perhaps a warning.

Ivy hesitated at the threshold, listening. The air felt alive, humming with something she couldn't quite name. Then a breeze stirred her curls and brushed against her cheek like a soft, invisible hand.

At that exact moment she heard a most curious sound—the faintest whisper, carried on the wind.

"Come, child..."

Her heart quickened, but fear did not take hold. Instead, she smiled. "Alright then," she whispered back to the wind, taking her first step into the Hollow. "Let's see what you've been hiding from me."

The mist swallowed her whole as the trees closed in, their branches arching overhead like the vaulted ceilings of a cathedral. Somewhere deep within the forest, the whispering wind laughed, carrying Ivy deeper into its secrets.

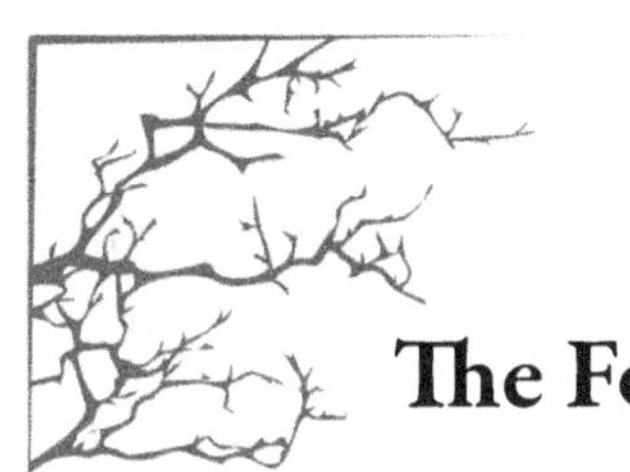

The Forest Beckons

The forest welcomed Ivy in a whispering symphony—a breeze that swept through golden birch leaves, carrying the scent of wet moss, pine needles, and something sweeter, like wild honey. She inhaled deeply, feeling the cool air fill her lungs. It smelled like autumn in all its wild, untamed glory.

As she stepped deeper into the Hollow, the mist thickened and the trees seemed to shift, rearranging themselves behind her. Ivy glanced over her shoulder to find the path she'd taken already obscured by twisting roots and shadowed ferns. It was as though the forest were folding in on itself, drawing her toward its heart.

She pressed on, brushing away stray branches and letting the soft earth cushion her steps. The forest felt alive—ancient and aware, as if it had been waiting for her. The wind carried fragments of melody, snatches of song without words, just on the edge of hearing.

A flicker of light caught her eye—a tiny glow dancing among the branches like a lantern on the wing. Ivy paused, tilting her head to watch. It bobbed and darted, beckoning her forward.

"A will-o'-wisp," she whispered, though she wasn't sure if she believed in such things.

The glowing light drifted deeper into the forest, and Ivy followed, her heart quickening. With every step, the trees seemed to hum—soft and low, as if they were murmuring secrets to one another. The air shimmered with something not quite visible, like threads of moonlight woven through the leaves.

Just as the last hint of daylight faded, a figure slinked from the underbrush—slender and quick as a shadow. Ivy gasped as a **fox** stepped into her path, its coat a gleaming mix of russet and gold, like the embers of a dying fire. Its amber eyes gleamed with mischief as it regarded her.

"Lost already?" the fox said, its voice light and full of teasing. "The forest enjoys swallowing curious little humans, you know."

Ivy blinked, startled. "You can talk?"

The fox grinned—if a fox could grin—and sat back on its haunches. "Of course. But only to those the wind favors." It swished its tail, a slow, deliberate movement. "You're not the first to wander here, you know. Most don't make it far."

"I'm not wandering," Ivy replied, lifting her chin. "I'm looking for something."

The fox's amber eyes narrowed with amusement. "Ah, looking. That's how it always begins, isn't it?" It circled her, its paws silent on the mossy ground. "And what is it you seek, little wanderer?"

Ivy hesitated, clutching the folded map in her coat pocket. "I'm looking for answers—about my grandmother. She had... a connection to this forest."

The fox's ears twitched. "Liora Brightwater," it murmured, tasting the name as if it were a sweet berry. "Yes, I remember her. She was a friend of the wind, that one."

"You knew her?" Ivy's voice was soft with disbelief, hope stirring in her chest. The fox flicked its tail. "I know many things. But that doesn't mean I'll share them."

Before Ivy could ask more, the fox leapt lightly onto a rock, its amber gaze sharp and knowing. "If you go any further, you'll meet the forest folk. They may not be as kind as I am."

"Kind?" Ivy repeated, raising an eyebrow.

The fox chuckled, a sound like dry leaves skittering across stone. "Consider my warning a kindness. Turn back now, little wanderer, before the forest takes a liking to you."

But Ivy stood her ground, determination burning in her chest. "I have to go on. I'm not afraid."

The fox tilted its head, studying her with an expression she couldn't quite read. Then it let out a sigh, as if amused by her stubbornness. "Very well," it said, leaping gracefully from the rock. "But don't say I didn't warn you." With that, it vanished into the underbrush, leaving only a faint scent of rain and earth behind.

The forest grew deeper, darker, and stranger. Moonlight filtered through the canopy in thin, silvery beams, casting shadows that danced with a life of their own. Ivy's breath clouded in the cool night air as she followed the path that seemed to reveal itself step by step, like a riddle unfolding.

Looking down she noticed something both odd and magical, nestled among the roots of an ancient oak were **mushroom houses**, their caps glowing softly in hues of blue and green. Tiny windows carved into the stems revealed flickering lights within, and delicate chimneys puffed out wisps of lavender-scented smoke.

Ivy knelt beside one of the houses, marveling at its intricate design—every detail carefully crafted, from the tiny flowerpot on the windowsill to the miniature broom leaning against the door.

A soft flutter of wings broke the stillness, and Ivy looked up just in time to see two figures no taller than her hand hovering in the air. **Fairies**—one with hair like golden silk, the other with wild curls the color of autumn leaves. Their wings shimmered like dragonfly wings, catching the moonlight with every beat.

The first fairy crossed her arms, her expression wary. "Humans don't belong in Windspindle Hollow," she said. The second fairy grinned mischievously. "Unless they bring sweets."

"I have blackberry jam," Ivy offered, holding up the jar from her satchel. The mischievous fairy brightened. "See? She's not so bad." The first fairy huffed, though a smile tugged at the corner of her mouth. "I'm **Tansy**," she said reluctantly. "And that troublemaker is my brother, **Thistle**."

"Pleasure to meet you," Thistle said with a flourish, performing a mid-air somersault. "We don't get many visitors—especially not humans."

"I'm Ivy," she replied. "I'm looking for... answers. About my grandmother, Liora." The fairies exchanged a glance, their wings buzzing softly. "Liora," Tansy whispered, her voice suddenly softer. "She was a friend of the forest."

"She kept the Hollow safe," Thistle added, perching on a mushroom cap. "But something changed. The magic's been... restless since she left." Ivy's heart ached with the weight of unspoken truths. "I need to understand what happened," she said.

Tansy fluttered closer, her expression solemn. "If you want answers, you'll have to go deeper—into the heart of the Hollow."

"But be careful," Thistle warned, his grin fading. "Not everything here is friendly."

"Especially not the shadows," Tansy added quietly. The fairies' words settled over Ivy like a shiver, but she squared her shoulders. She had come too far to turn back now.

Streams That Sing

The deeper Ivy wandered into Windspindle Hollow, the more alive the forest became. Strange flowers with silver petals glowed softly beneath the brush, and mushrooms hummed a low, rhythmic melody, as if the ground itself was singing an ancient lullaby.

The trees whispered to one another in languages Ivy could not understand, their leaves shimmering as though laced with stardust. She could feel it now—this forest had a pulse, slow and steady, as if the entire Hollow was one great heart, beating quietly under the weight of centuries.

Tansy and Thistle flitted around Ivy like mischievous sparks, occasionally darting off to inspect some luminous plant or oddly shaped rock. They spoke in hushed tones about the forest's magic, offering bits of cryptic advice that seemed only half helpful. "Step lightly," Tansy warned, "or the forest will remember your weight."

"Keep your eyes open," Thistle added, "but never trust what they see." Ivy glanced at the path ahead, where shadows stretched long and thin in the fading light. The way was winding and uncertain, as though the forest refused to reveal its true layout all at once. She tightened her grip on the strap of her satchel, her pulse quickening. Though there was a thrill to the magic that buzzed in the air, there was also something unsettling—like standing on the edge of a dream that could turn into a nightmare at any moment.

The fox had warned her. But Ivy wasn't turning back. A cool breeze brushed her cheek, carrying a sound that made her heart skip—a melody, soft and lilting, like a lullaby sung by water. It drifted on the wind, pulling at her, tugging her deeper into the forest. It was a song without words, yet it seemed familiar, like a half-remembered tune from a dream.

"What is that?" Ivy whispered, glancing at Tansy and Thistle. "The stream," Tansy replied, her voice unusually solemn. "It sings sometimes. It knows things."

"It doesn't sing for everyone," Thistle added, tilting his head toward Ivy. "It likes you." Ivy wasn't sure if that was comforting or unsettling. "What does it know?" she asked. Thistle shrugged. "Oh, lots of things. Lost things. Forgotten things. Sometimes it sings secrets."

Without another word, Ivy followed the melody. The fairies flitted after her, their wings buzzing softly in the twilight. The song grew clearer as they moved deeper into the forest, and soon they reached the edge of a stream that wound like a silver ribbon through the undergrowth.

The water shimmered, catching the light of the rising moon, and as Ivy knelt beside it, she noticed that the surface was strangely still—too still, as though the water was waiting for something. She dipped her hand into the cool stream, and the moment her fingers touched the surface, the world shifted.

The forest around her blurred, and Ivy found herself standing in a different time, a different place. The stream was still there, but the woods looked younger, greener—untouched by the creeping darkness she had felt earlier. In the clearing ahead, two figures stood beneath the light of a full moon.

Ivy's breath caught in her throat as she recognized one of them: **Liora Brightwater**, her grandmother. She looked younger than Ivy remembered, her silver hair streaked with auburn, her face alight with quiet wisdom. She wore a simple cloak fastened with a silver brooch, and in her hands, she held a small vial filled with glowing liquid.

Beside her stood another figure—a woman draped in shadows, her face obscured by the hood of a deep blue cloak. **The Hollow Witch.** Moonlight glinted off her fingers, long and pale, as she accepted the vial from Liora.

"I can only hold it back for so long," the witch said, her voice low and musical, like wind through chimes. "The forest needs a new guardian. If it goes untended, the shadows will take root." Liora nodded, her expression grave. "I'll find someone," she promised. "The magic won't fade."

The witch's gaze softened, though there was a sadness in her eyes that Ivy couldn't quite place. "Not all magic is meant to last," she whispered. "But while it does, we guard it."

The vision shimmered, the edges blurring like ripples across the surface of a pond. Ivy reached out, wanting to call out to her grandmother, but the scene dissolved before she could speak. The forest returned around her, and the stream hummed softly beneath her hand, as if satisfied with the memory it had shared.

Ivy sat back on her heels, her heart racing. The vision had felt so real, like stepping into a forgotten dream. She knew now that her grandmother had not only been connected to the Hollow—she had been entrusted with its care. And there was something urgent in the witch's words, something that made Ivy's skin prickle with unease.

The forest needed a guardian.

Tansy and Thistle hovered nearby, watching her with curious expressions. "You saw something, didn't you?" Tansy asked softly. Ivy nodded, still catching her breath. "It was my grandmother," she whispered. "She was with the witch. They were... guarding something."

The fairies exchanged a glance, their wings flickering nervously. "If the witch spoke to Liora," Tansy said, "then the forest must have chosen her. The Hollow doesn't trust just anyone." "But it's been restless since she left," Thistle added. "Without a guardian, the magic starts to unravel."

Ivy's stomach churned. She hadn't expected this—hadn't expected to find herself standing on the edge of something so vast, so ancient. She had only wanted to understand her grandmother's life, but now it seemed that life had been tied to a responsibility far greater than Ivy could have imagined.

The wind stirred again, rustling the leaves overhead, and Ivy thought she heard a whisper woven into the breeze. *"Come, child... the heart of the Hollow waits."*

She took a deep breath and stood, brushing dirt from her knees. "I need to find the witch," she said, determination hardening in her chest. "If the forest needs a guardian, I have to know what that means." Tansy's wings buzzed anxiously. "The witch isn't easy to find. She's... hidden. Some say she only appears to those the forest chooses."

"Well," Ivy said, gripping the strap of her satchel, "the forest brought me this far. I'll take my chances." The path ahead grew darker, the trees clustering tightly together, their branches forming tangled arches above the stream. Ivy followed the water, letting its soft hum guide her deeper into the Hollow. Shadows flickered at the edges of her vision—shapes that seemed almost human, but when she turned to look, they dissolved into mist.

The fairies whispered nervously as they flew beside her. "The shadows are watching," Tansy murmured. "We should turn back." But Ivy shook her head. "Not yet. We're close—I can feel it."

The stream twisted sharply, and as Ivy rounded the bend, she found herself standing in front of a **massive oak tree** that rose like a tower from the forest floor. Its bark was knotted with age, and its roots curled into the earth like ancient fingers. Nestled among the branches was a **treehouse**, its windows glowing faintly with soft, golden light.

Ivy's breath caught in her throat. "The treehouse library," she whispered. Thistle grinned. "Told you the forest liked you."

They flew ahead, disappearing through one of the open windows. Ivy followed, climbing the spiral staircase that wound around the trunk. As she reached the top, the scent of parchment and old wood greeted her, and she stepped into a room filled with **bookshelves** carved from the tree itself.

In the center of the room stood a **sprite** with golden wings that shimmered in the lamplight. His eyes were wise and ancient, and a gentle smile curved his lips as he regarded Ivy.

"Welcome, Ivy Brightwater," the sprite said. "I am **Eldwyn**, keeper of the library." Ivy swallowed, feeling a strange sense of belonging settle over her. "You know who I am?" Eldwyn nodded. "The forest remembers your grandmother well. And now, it remembers you."

Ivy glanced around the library, her heart racing with the weight of everything she had discovered. "I need answers," she said softly. "About my grandmother. About the witch. And about the magic in this forest."

Eldwyn's smile deepened. "All answers come in time," he said. "But the first thing you must understand is this: magic is not just something you carry. It is something you become." Ivy's breath hitched. "What do you mean?"

Eldwyn gestured toward a **book bound in green leather** that rested on a nearby table. "Your grandmother's notes," he said. "They will tell you what you need to know."

Ivy approached the book, her fingers trembling slightly as she opened it. The pages were filled with her grandmother's neat, looping handwriting, sketches of plants and charms, and spells woven with poetry.

AND THERE, ON THE VERY last page, was a single sentence that made Ivy's heart stop:

"The forest chooses, and what is chosen cannot walk away."

Ivy closed the book slowly, the weight of those words settling over her like a blanket of stars. She knew then that she was standing on the threshold of something far greater than herself. And there would be no turning back.

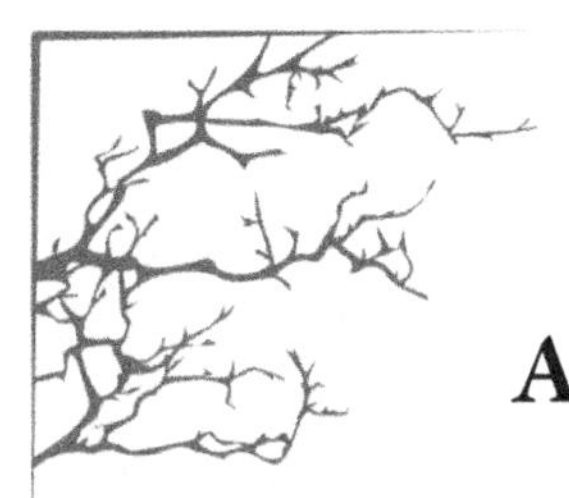

A Dance with
Shadows

Ivy traced the final sentence in her grandmother's journal with trembling fingers: *"The forest chooses, and what is chosen cannot walk away."* It felt like a thread pulling tight, binding her to something ancient, something deep within the heart of the Hollow.

Her breath clouded in the cool air of the treehouse, the weight of her discovery settling heavy on her chest. Whatever magic Liora had been part of, it was now unraveling—and the forest had brought Ivy here to take up the threads.

Behind her, Eldwyn's wings fluttered softly as he pulled a book from the shelf, its pages rustling like leaves. "If the forest has chosen you, Ivy Brightwater," the sprite said, "then it will reveal more as you journey deeper. But you must tread carefully. The magic here is old, and not all of it welcomes change."

Ivy glanced down at her grandmother's journal again. The words felt like both a warning and a promise, etched in ink that seemed to shimmer faintly in the low light of the treehouse.

"I don't have a choice, do I?" she whispered.

Eldwyn smiled gently, a knowing glimmer in his ancient eyes. "None of us do, once the forest calls."

Ivy descended from the treehouse, the wind brushing through her curls, carrying the scent of damp wood and the faintest hint of lavender. The fairies, Tansy and Thistle, hovered beside her, their wings buzzing anxiously.

"You're really going to find the witch?" Thistle asked, somersaulting through the air as if to mask his nerves. "She's... not exactly friendly, you know."

"I don't think I have much of a choice," Ivy replied. "The forest needs a guardian, and I need to know the truth about my grandmother."

Tansy landed on Ivy's shoulder, her tiny hands gripping a curl of Ivy's hair. "The witch isn't evil," she murmured, "but she isn't easy, either. You'll have to be careful."

Ivy nodded, clutching the strap of her satchel. The stream still hummed softly at her side, its waters glinting silver under the moonlight, as if guiding her toward something just out of reach. The shadows between the trees seemed to pulse with quiet life, shifting and swirling at the edges of her vision. She took a step forward—and the forest changed.

The air thickened, the trees tightening around her like the bars of a cage. The path twisted in unnatural ways, leading her in spirals that made her head swim. The lantern-like mushrooms that had glowed softly before now flickered with uncertainty, casting jittery light across the forest floor. The stream's melody faltered, notes breaking and scattering like lost dreams.

And the shadows—oh, the shadows danced.

Shapes moved in the corners of Ivy's vision, flitting between the trunks like restless spirits. She could feel their gaze, cold and curious, brushing against her skin like a winter wind. Every time she turned to look, they dissolved into mist, only to reappear just beyond her sight, shifting, waiting.

"What do they want?" Ivy whispered, her voice barely audible. Tansy perched on her shoulder, her wings quivering. "They want the magic," she said softly. "They're drawn to it—hungry for it. And without a guardian to keep them at bay..."

"They'll take everything," Thistle finished grimly, circling Ivy protectively. "Even you, if you're not careful."

Ivy swallowed hard, feeling the weight of their words settle over her. But she knew, deep down, that she couldn't turn back now. She had come too far, and the forest had chosen her. Whatever awaited at the heart of the Hollow, she would have to face it.

The wind shifted, carrying a faint, familiar scent—lavender and thyme, just like her grandmother's herb garden. Ivy's heart ached at the memory, but it also gave her strength. She straightened her shoulders and took another step forward, deeper into the forest.

The shadows hissed, swirling faster now, drawn to her movement like moths to flame. Ivy could feel them pressing closer, a cold weight at her back, but she didn't stop. She followed the stream as it wound through the darkened woods, its song faltering but persistent.

Then, just ahead, she saw it—a glimmer of light, soft and steady, like a beacon in the night. Ivy quickened her pace, the shadows clawing at her heels, and burst into a small, moonlit clearing.

At the center of the clearing stood an ancient stone well, draped in ivy and glowing faintly under the light of the full moon. The air here felt different—still and sacred, as though time itself had paused to watch. And standing beside the well, her cloak trailing like smoke, was **the Hollow Witch**.

Her presence was both beautiful and terrifying, a figure woven from twilight and moonlight, her face hidden beneath a hood stitched with tiny stars. Ivy could feel the weight of her gaze, even though she couldn't see the witch's eyes.

"You've come," the witch said softly, her voice a melody that echoed through the clearing. "Just as I knew you would."

Ivy took a step forward, her heart pounding. "You knew my grandmother," she whispered. "You trusted her. And now... I think the forest has chosen me."

The witch tilted her head, a faint smile curving her lips. "It has," she said. "But being chosen is only the beginning. The forest needs more than a guardian—it needs someone willing to become part of it. Someone who understands that magic cannot be held, only tended. Are you willing to do that, Ivy Brightwater?"

Ivy hesitated, the weight of the witch's words settling over her like a heavy cloak. But she knew, deep in her bones, that this was what her grandmother had prepared her for all along.

"Yes," Ivy whispered. "I am."

The witch's smile deepened, and she extended a pale hand toward Ivy. "Then let the dance begin."

In that moment, the shadows that had followed Ivy erupted into the clearing, swirling in a wild, chaotic frenzy. But the witch raised her hand, and the shadows stilled, drawn into a slow, rhythmic dance that matched the pulse of the forest.

Ivy stood at the edge of the clearing, watching as the witch moved gracefully through the shifting darkness, her cloak trailing like smoke on the wind. The shadows followed her lead, drawn into the dance, their sharp edges softening as they swayed and spun.

And then, without hesitation, Ivy stepped forward and joined the dance. The moment her feet touched the shadowed ground, she felt the magic of the forest surge through her—wild and ancient, like the roots of an old tree sinking deep into the earth. The shadows welcomed her, wrapping around her like silk, and for the first time, Ivy understood.

Magic was not something to possess—it was something to live. It was in the dance of shadows and moonlight, in the hum of streams and the whisper of leaves. It was in her heartbeat, in her breath, in every step she took.

As Ivy moved through the clearing, the shadows danced with her, their edges blurring into light. The witch watched, her smile soft and knowing, and when the dance finally ended, the clearing was silent once more.

The shadows had returned to the forest, their hunger sated, and the well glowed softly under the light of the full moon.

"You are ready," the witch said quietly, her voice full of pride. "The Hollow has chosen well."

Ivy stood still, catching her breath, her heart full of both wonder and certainty. She knew now that she belonged here—among the shadows and streams, the trees and the wind. She was not just a visitor to the forest; she was part of it, as her grandmother had been before her.

And she would protect it, no matter what.

The witch nodded once, a silent farewell, and then she dissolved into moonlight, leaving Ivy standing alone in the clearing. But Ivy didn't feel alone.

The forest hummed with quiet joy, and the wind whispered a welcome only she could hear.

The Gnome
Blacksmith's Gift

The moon hung low over Windspindle Hollow, its silvery light spilling like water over the forest floor. Ivy stood alone in the clearing where the witch had vanished, her heart still thrumming with the rhythm of the shadow-dance. The forest around her was quieter now, the hum of magic settling into the earth like a deep breath. But she knew the journey was far from over.

Windspindle Hollow had chosen her, and that choice carried a weight—a responsibility that she could feel in her bones. The night was far from over, and the magic that whispered through the trees called her onward. Somewhere deeper in the forest was a blacksmith, one who could help her understand the strange silver pendant the gnome had spoken of in her grandmother's notes.

Clutching her satchel, Ivy stepped back into the shadows of the woods, letting the soft hum of the stream guide her. Tansy and Thistle zipped ahead, their wings glowing faintly in the dark. They spoke in quick bursts, half-excited and half-nervous, as if eager to be moving again but wary of the forest's mood.

"You know the way to the blacksmith, don't you?" Ivy asked. "Of course we do!" Thistle chirped, darting through a beam of moonlight. "He lives under the great oak, near the glade where the fireflies dance."

"But we don't visit often," Tansy added, her voice quieter. "He... doesn't like visitors."

"Why not?" Ivy asked, stepping over a tangle of roots. Thistle grinned mischievously. "He's a gnome. They're all a bit cranky."

As they ventured deeper into the forest, the air grew warmer, scented with iron and woodsmoke. Ivy's footsteps softened against a path of moss, and soon she saw it—a **massive oak tree**, its gnarled roots twisting deep into the earth like the veins of the forest itself. Nestled beneath the roots was a workshop, its entrance marked by a round wooden door bound with iron. The door stood ajar, and from within came the steady clang of metal striking metal.

Ivy approached cautiously, the fairies fluttering nervously beside her. "Are you sure we should be here?" Tansy whispered.

But before Ivy could answer, a voice echoed from within the workshop, gruff and impatient. "Well, don't just stand there gawking! If you've come for trouble, best be on with it. If you've come for business, speak your piece!" Ivy hesitated, then stepped through the door into the gnome's workshop.

The interior was a wonderland of metal and magic. **Silver leaves**, each etched with intricate runes, hung from the ceiling like wind chimes. Tools of all kinds lay scattered across wooden benches—hammers, tongs, and strange contraptions Ivy couldn't begin to name. In the center of it all stood the **gnome blacksmith** himself, a stout figure with wiry white hair and a beard that nearly reached the ground. He wore a leather apron stained with soot, and his eyes sparkled like embers as he looked Ivy up and down.

"Well, well," the gnome muttered, rubbing his beard. "Liora Brightwater's kin, eh? I thought I smelled old magic on you." Ivy blinked in surprise. "You knew my grandmother?"

"Knew her?" The gnome let out a huff of laughter. "She was one of the few humans worth knowing. A good soul, that one. Always brought me fresh herbs for my tea." He eyed her closely, his gaze sharp. "So, what brings you here, girl? You didn't come all this way just to reminisce about the old days."

Ivy reached into her satchel and pulled out the silver **pendant**—the one she'd found tucked in her grandmother's journal. It glinted softly in the firelight, the runes along its surface faintly glowing. "I found this," she said, holding it out to him. "It feels... important."

The gnome took the pendant carefully, turning it over in his hands. His eyes narrowed as he studied the runes. "Ah, this is one of my pieces," he muttered. "Didn't think I'd see it again."

"You made it?" Ivy asked.

The gnome nodded. "Aye. Liora commissioned it from me years ago, back when the forest first started stirring. This pendant is more than just pretty metal—it's a **focus**. Strengthens magic, binds spells tighter. Your grandmother was preparing for something big, that much I know."

"She knew the forest would need a new guardian," Ivy said softly. The gnome nodded, his expression solemn. "Aye. And it looks like that someone's you."

The gnome handed the pendant back to Ivy, his gaze serious. "If you're going to take up Liora's mantle, you'll need more than just that trinket. You'll need a proper tool."

"A tool?" Ivy asked, confused.

"A **weapon, of sorts.** Not one for fighting, mind you, but for channeling the forest's magic," the gnome explained. He motioned toward a corner of the workshop, where a bundle of silver and oakwood lay wrapped in cloth. "I've been working on this for years, waiting for the right moment."

With a grunt, the gnome unwrapped the bundle to reveal a **staff**, its shaft carved from dark oak and inlaid with silver runes that glowed faintly in the dim light. At its top, a small, hollow sphere rested, as if waiting to hold something precious.

"The pendant fits here," the gnome said, pointing to the hollow sphere. "Once it's set, the staff will become your anchor to the Hollow's magic."

Ivy hesitated, running her fingers over the smooth wood. "What if I'm not ready?" she whispered.

The gnome shrugged. "None of us are ever truly ready for what the forest asks of us. But we learn. And you've got more of your grandmother in you than you realize."

Tansy and Thistle fluttered closer, their wings buzzing softly. "It's beautiful," Tansy whispered. Thistle grinned. "I bet it could make lightning. Or summon storms!"

The gnome let out a chuckle. "It'll do what it needs to do, lad. But only if Ivy learns to wield it properly."

With the pendant nestled into the staff's hollow sphere, Ivy felt a strange warmth flow through her—like the first sip of tea on a cold morning or the comfort of a favorite book. The staff hummed softly in her hands, as though recognizing her touch.

"It's yours now," the gnome said. "Take care of it, and it'll take care of you." Ivy nodded, her heart full of both fear and excitement. She knew this was just the beginning of her journey, and there was still so much to learn. But for the first time since entering the Hollow, she felt... ready.

"Thank you," she whispered, clutching the staff tightly. The gnome gave a gruff nod. "Don't mention it. Just don't go losing that pendant—it's the key to everything."

As Ivy stepped out of the workshop and back into the forest, the air felt different—lighter, as if the Hollow had been holding its breath and was now exhaling softly. The trees swayed gently in the breeze, their leaves shimmering like stars.

"Well," Thistle said, darting around Ivy's head. "What's next?" Ivy smiled, lifting the staff and feeling its warmth pulse through her. "Next," she said, "we find the heart of the Hollow."

"And then?" Tansy asked, her tiny voice full of curiosity. Ivy looked out at the forest, her heart steady. "Then we protect it."

The wind stirred the leaves, carrying a soft whisper through the trees—a promise, a welcome, and a challenge all at once. Ivy knew that the path ahead would not be easy. But with the staff in her hands and the forest at her back, she was ready to face whatever lay ahead.

The heart of Windspindle Hollow was waiting. And Ivy Brightwater was ready to answer its call.

A Moonlit Trial

The forest stretched endlessly ahead, and with each step Ivy felt the weight of the staff in her hands like a heartbeat in tune with the Hollow. Tansy and Thistle danced through the air, flickering orbs of light that whispered encouragement, but Ivy could feel the forest shifting again. Something stirred—something old, testing her resolve.

As the path ahead darkened, Ivy sensed the magic surrounding her shifting from warm invitation to something sharper, colder. The trees thickened, their branches weaving together into tight arches that blocked out the moonlight, casting the forest floor in shadow. The comforting hum of the stream faded behind her, replaced by a silence that felt too complete—like the forest was holding its breath.

"Are you sure we're going the right way?" Tansy whispered, her voice barely audible. Ivy gripped the staff tighter, the runes along its oak shaft glowing softly under her touch. "I can feel it," she whispered back. "The heart of the Hollow is near."

Thistle zipped in front of her, hovering just above the ground. "Near is one thing. Getting there is another." His playful tone faltered, replaced by unease. "The forest doesn't just *let* you reach the heart. There's always a trial."

"A trial?" Ivy echoed, slowing her steps.

Tansy landed lightly on Ivy's shoulder, her wings trembling. "The forest tests those who seek the heart," she explained. "It needs to know you're worthy. It wants to be sure you won't harm the magic you've sworn to protect."

"Or let it fall into the wrong hands," Thistle added grimly. Ivy stopped, her heart racing. She looked down at the staff, its silver runes shimmering faintly in the dark, and then back at the dense forest ahead. "What kind of trial?" she asked.

Tansy exchanged a glance with Thistle, and her tiny voice dropped into a serious whisper. "No one knows. The forest shows you what you fear most, what you doubt, what you love. If you fail the trial, it won't let you reach the heart."

"And what happens if I succeed?" Ivy asked, her throat tight. Thistle gave a crooked grin, though there was little humor in it. "Then you *become* the heart."

They continued deeper into the Hollow, where the air grew heavier and colder, as if winter had arrived early. Ivy's boots crunched over frost-kissed leaves, and the scent of pine mingled with something sharper—like old iron and damp stone. The path twisted and turned, narrowing until Ivy had to push through tangled branches that clawed at her cloak.

And then, just ahead, she saw it: a **clearing bathed in moonlight**, surrounded by towering blackthorn trees. In the center stood a **stone circle**, weathered and ancient, its surface marked with runes that pulsed faintly under the light of the full moon.

"The trial begins here," Tansy whispered, her wings buzzing nervously. Thistle landed on Ivy's shoulder, unusually quiet. "We can't follow you into this one, Ivy. Whatever you see in the circle—it's for you alone."

Ivy's heart pounded in her chest, but she gave the fairies a small, determined nod. "I can do this." With that, she stepped into the stone circle.

The moment her foot touched the stones, the forest around her vanished. Ivy stood in a place that felt both familiar and strange—her grandmother's cottage, but not quite. The windows were dark, the air heavy with the scent of rain, and the hearth lay cold and empty. Ivy's breath fogged the air as she took a step forward, her boots creaking on the old wooden floor.

"Grandmother?" she called softly, her voice echoing through the stillness. No answer came, only the distant sound of a storm gathering on the horizon. The walls of the cottage seemed to close in, shifting and twisting like the branches of the forest. Ivy's heart tightened with unease. This was not a memory—it was something else. A reflection, perhaps. A warning. And then she saw her.

A figure stood by the hearth, shrouded in shadow, her face hidden beneath a dark hood. **The Hollow Witch.** But this time, her presence was not gentle. There was no soft smile, no knowing gaze—only darkness, cold and complete.

"You think you can take her place?" the witch hissed, her voice sharp as broken glass. "You think you can carry the weight of this magic? Foolish girl."

"I'm not afraid," Ivy whispered, though her hands shook as she clutched the staff tighter. The witch stepped closer, her shadow stretching across the floor like smoke. "Not afraid? Then why do your hands tremble? Why does your heart race?"

The staff hummed softly in Ivy's grip, the runes flickering in and out of light. She forced herself to meet the witch's gaze, though fear clawed at her chest. "Because this matters," she whispered. "Because I care. And that's why I won't fail."

The witch's shadow twisted and writhed, shifting into the shapes of all Ivy's doubts—visions of her grandmother's disappointed gaze, of the villagers whispering behind her back, of the forest collapsing under the weight of her mistakes. The air grew cold, sharp as ice, and the room seemed to tilt beneath her feet.

But Ivy held her ground. She closed her eyes, breathing deeply, and let the hum of the staff's magic steady her. She knew now that this trial wasn't about fear—it was about trust. Trusting herself. Trusting the forest. Trusting the magic that had chosen her.

"I am not my doubts," Ivy whispered into the darkness. "I am not my fears." The witch's shadow wavered, flickering like the flame of a dying candle.

"I am Ivy Brightwater," she said, her voice growing stronger. "And I will protect this forest. I will carry this magic. I will not walk away."

The shadows dissolved, and the air around her shifted. The cold lifted, replaced by a warm breeze that smelled of lavender and rain. The cottage faded, and Ivy found herself standing once more in the stone circle, the moonlight soft and welcoming on her skin.

Tansy and Thistle hovered just outside the circle, their faces full of nervous hope. "Did you do it?" Thistle asked eagerly. "Did you pass?" Ivy smiled, lifting the staff as its runes glowed brighter than ever. "I did."

The fairies cheered, their wings buzzing with joy, and the forest around them seemed to hum in approval, as though welcoming Ivy home.

As they left the clearing, the wind carried a new whisper through the trees—a promise, soft and sure. The heart of the Hollow waited, and Ivy knew now that she was ready to meet it.

She was no longer just a visitor in this forest. She was its guardian. Its heart.

And Windspindle Hollow had found its keeper once more.

The Shadows Gather

The path through the forest grew strange and uncertain, as if the earth beneath Ivy's boots was shifting like a restless dream. Branches bent low, heavy with moonlight, and leaves whispered secrets she could almost—but not quite—understand. The hum of the forest, usually warm and familiar, had grown quiet, as though the woods were holding their breath.

Above her, the stars spilled across the sky in shimmering rivers, distant and cold, casting faint silver upon the twisted roots and damp earth. Ivy tightened her grip on the staff, feeling its magic pulse in response, a soft, rhythmic thrum that seemed to say: *Keep going. You are not alone.*

Then, through the thick canopy, something ancient stirred—so quiet it might have been mistaken for the shift of wind through branches. But it was not the wind. It was the *presence* that lived between the trees, watching, waiting, patient as shadow.

A low murmur, just at the edge of hearing, brushed the back of Ivy's thoughts. She felt the forest shift, as if a great weight was sliding into place, blocking her path forward. It wasn't a sound she noticed at first—it was absence. No more distant song of the stream. No more whispers from the wind. The Hollow had gone still, like a sleeping giant stirring toward wakefulness.

The shadows, quiet and deliberate, began to gather. It started with a flicker—a movement just beyond her sight, where the light could not reach. Shapes took form in the periphery, gliding along the edges of moonlight as though made from the fabric of forgotten dreams. The cool air thickened with their presence, and the forest seemed to bow beneath them, yielding to something older and darker than Ivy had ever known.

The shadows did not attack. They circled slowly, closing the distance between themselves and Ivy, as if curious—hungry, but not hurried. Their edges whispered like dry leaves, shifting between forms: human-like silhouettes, shifting animals, and spiraling tendrils of smoke. They did not need to move fast. The weight of their presence alone was enough to make Ivy's heart stutter.

Tansy and Thistle fluttered close, their glow dimming with fear. "We have to move," Tansy whispered, her voice thin and urgent, like wind rattling through hollow reeds.

"They'll trap us here if we wait too long," Thistle added, darting nervously around Ivy's head.

Ivy's heart thrummed in time with the pulse of the staff, steady and insistent, and for a moment she closed her eyes, centering herself. She could feel the pull of the heart of the Hollow—it was near, not far now, just beyond the dark veil of the shadows. But the shadows could sense it too.

They wanted what she carried. They wanted the magic bound within the oak and silver. They wanted *her*. The first shadow slipped closer, a curling wisp of darkness that brushed Ivy's cheek like cold breath. She stepped back, but the shadows were closing in, filling the air with a low, buzzing hum, like the murmur of voices long forgotten.

Not a single sound was clear, but the meaning was unmistakable: *Give it to us. Let us in. Let go, and we will carry the burden instead.*

Ivy gripped the staff tighter. "No." Her voice was low, but steady. The shadows quivered, then reformed, becoming taller, thicker, as though fed by her resistance. They began to swirl, forming a dark cyclone around Ivy, blurring the edges of the forest, pulling at her thoughts with tendrils of doubt and fear. The staff's light flickered, dimming under the weight of their presence. Ivy's breath caught.

But then—like a lantern flickering back to life—a sound rose in the distance. It began as a whisper, barely more than a breeze threading through the leaves. But soon it gathered strength, lifting into a melody that curled through the trees like the first light of dawn. A **song**, soft and ancient, carried on the wind, stirring the air with notes that felt like home.

The stream's voice had returned. It sang not in words but in memory, in the language of water and stone, of roots that reached deep into the earth and branches that stretched toward the sky. The song wound through Ivy's chest, filling her with warmth, washing away the cold tendrils of fear that the shadows had planted.

And in that moment, the staff pulsed again—once, twice—its silver runes glowing brighter, as if drinking in the song. Ivy felt its power rise through her hands, steady and patient, like the strength of roots holding fast against a storm.

With a deep breath, she lifted the staff. "You cannot have this," she whispered, the magic blooming through her words like a wildflower opening under sunlight.

The shadows hissed, recoiling as the light from the staff spread outward, soft and radiant, pushing them back inch by inch. They writhed against it, twisting and shrinking, their shapes unraveling like mist at dawn. But still, they lingered—testing, waiting for a falter, a crack in her resolve.

The forest hummed around her, the song of the stream rising and falling, and Ivy knew what she needed to do. **The forest had chosen her, but now it was time for her to choose it.**

She closed her eyes and let herself fall into the magic. Not as a burden to carry, but as a river she would swim in—a thread she would weave into the fabric of herself, binding her heart to the Hollow's forever.

And the staff responded. Light burst from its runes, flowing outward like water, filling every crevice of the forest. The shadows shrieked, their forms scattering into shards of darkness that melted into the earth. The air cleared, light and warm again, and the weight of the shadows lifted, leaving only the quiet hum of the Hollow behind.

When Ivy opened her eyes, the forest stood still once more—calm, serene, as though nothing had ever disturbed it. The path ahead stretched clear under the light of the moon, and in the distance, she could feel it:

The heart of the Hollow, waiting for her. Tansy let out a breathy cheer, her tiny wings buzzing with relief. "You did it!" she whispered.

Thistle spun in dizzy circles, giddy with excitement. "I thought they'd swallow us whole! But you—*you* burned them up like fireflies!"

Ivy smiled, though her hands still trembled slightly from the magic's weight. "It wasn't just me," she said softly. "The forest—*it helped.*"

And in that moment, she knew the forest would always help her, so long as she listened—so long as she trusted the magic that thrived in every stream, every leaf, every root.

Brindle the Fox appeared at the edge of the path, his amber eyes gleaming in the moonlight. "Well," he said, his voice light with amusement, "you've certainly made an impression."

Ivy let out a soft laugh, her heart feeling lighter than it had in days. "Is that your way of saying you're proud of me?"

Brindle tilted his head. "Something like that." Then, with a flick of his tail, he added, "Come on, little guardian. The heart won't wait forever."

With Tansy and Thistle flitting beside her, and Brindle leading the way, Ivy took a deep breath and stepped forward. The forest welcomed her, the trees parting gently as she passed, their leaves shimmering under the light of the moon.

And as the magic pulsed through her staff, steady and true, Ivy knew with quiet certainty that she had become what the Hollow needed.

The heart of the forest was hers to protect now, and whatever lay ahead—she was ready.

The Witch's Truth

The air grew softer as Ivy followed Brindle along the path that wound toward the **heart of the Hollow**. The trees, which had bent low and gnarled before, now rose tall and straight, their branches arching overhead like the vaults of a cathedral. A gentle light filtered through the canopy, not from the moon but from the forest itself—soft glimmers that floated like drifting stars, casting pools of silver across the ground.

With every step, Ivy felt the magic pulse stronger beneath her skin. It thrummed in her veins like a second heartbeat, as though the forest and her body were merging into one rhythm. Tansy and Thistle fluttered beside her in a dance of quiet awe, their usual chatter subdued in the presence of such deep magic.

Brindle the Fox glanced back, his amber eyes catching the light like embers. "We're close," he murmured. "Do you feel it? The heart is calling to you."

Ivy nodded, clutching her staff tighter. "Yes. It feels... like it's waiting." Brindle gave a small, knowing grin. "It is. And so is she."

Ivy's pulse quickened at the fox's words. She knew now whom he meant—the **Hollow Witch**, the figure who had haunted her visions and dreams since she'd entered the forest. The woman cloaked in shadows, tied to her grandmother's past, and to Ivy's own future.

The trees ahead parted slowly, revealing a **grove bathed in starlight**. At its center, a great tree rose—so ancient and wide it seemed to cradle the sky itself. Its roots twisted deep into the earth, while delicate, glowing blossoms sprouted along its massive branches, their petals shimmering with every shift of the breeze.

This was the **Heart of the Hollow**. Ivy knew it without question. And standing at the base of the tree, her cloak trailing like smoke, was the **Hollow Witch**.

The witch's presence was both beautiful and terrifying, like the sharp edge of a dream that lingers just beyond waking. Her hood no longer obscured her face—pale as moonlight, framed by black curls streaked with silver. Her eyes shimmered with sadness, as though she carried the weight of every secret the forest had ever known.

"You've come," the witch said softly, her voice a song woven from twilight. "Just as the forest knew you would." Ivy stepped forward, her breath catching in her chest. "You knew my grandmother," she whispered. "You were... close."

The witch gave a slow nod, her gaze never leaving Ivy's. "Liora was my dearest friend. More than that, she was my tether—my anchor to this world." The sadness in her voice deepened, like the low notes of a forgotten lullaby. "When she left, the forest began to unravel. It has waited for a new heart ever since." Ivy's throat tightened. "She didn't want to leave, did she?"

"No." The witch's voice dropped to a whisper, heavy with regret. "But life outside the Hollow pulls, just as magic within it binds. Liora's heart belonged in two places, and in the end, she had to choose."

The witch's eyes glimmered with unshed tears. "She chose you, Ivy. She left the forest behind so you could grow up in the world beyond it—so you could live a life free of this burden. But now, the choice must pass to you."

Ivy's chest ached with the weight of the witch's words. "And what if I choose the forest?" she whispered. "What happens then?"

The witch stepped closer, the hem of her cloak brushing the glowing petals beneath the great tree. "If you stay," she said, "you will become the Hollow's new guardian. Its magic will bind itself to you, and you will live as part of the forest—forever." Her voice softened. "You will never grow old, never leave, but you will also never return to the life you knew."

Ivy swallowed hard. "And if I leave?"

The witch's gaze turned distant, as though she were watching some far-off memory play out before her. "If you leave, the forest will remain—but only for a time. Without a guardian, the magic will fade, and the Hollow will become just another forest, its secrets forgotten, its life diminished."

Ivy's heart felt as though it were caught between two worlds—one foot in the forest, the other in the life she had left behind. She thought of her grandmother, of the sacrifice Liora had made to give her a life beyond the Hollow. And she thought of the magic she had found here, the quiet hum of the trees, the song of the stream, and the sense of belonging she had never felt anywhere else.

She looked down at the staff in her hands, the silver pendant nestled within its crown, glowing softly with the magic it held. This, too, was part of her now—just as the forest was part of her heart.

And then she knew. **The answer was not to hold on to one life or the other, but to find the place where both could exist together.**

With a deep breath, Ivy stepped toward the great tree, her hands steady on the staff. "I will be the guardian," she whispered, "but not in the way the forest expects."

The witch's brow furrowed. "What do you mean?" Ivy raised the staff, feeling its warmth bloom through her fingers. "The magic doesn't have to be trapped here. It can flow—between worlds, between lives. Just as the stream carries water to the forest and beyond, I will carry the magic with me, wherever I go."

The witch's expression softened, a flicker of hope kindling in her gaze. "You mean to walk both paths." Ivy smiled, her heart light and sure. "Yes. I will protect the Hollow—and live in the world beyond it. I will be its guardian, not by staying, but by carrying it with me."

The witch let out a soft laugh, like the sound of wind through leaves. "Liora would be proud of you." She reached forward, her hand resting briefly on Ivy's shoulder, and Ivy felt the magic of the forest flow through her—a soft, steady hum, like the roots of a tree stretching deep into the earth. The witch's presence shimmered, becoming light and air, dissolving into the petals of the great tree.

"You are ready," the witch whispered, her voice fading like the last notes of a lullaby. "The forest is yours now."

And with that, the Hollow Witch vanished, her form dissolving into moonlight, leaving Ivy standing beneath the ancient tree with the staff in her hands and the magic of the forest in her heart.

The Binding Ritual

The moment Ivy stepped beneath the branches of the **great heart-tree**, the air shimmered with ancient magic, weaving threads of moonlight through her thoughts. The ground beneath her feet pulsed gently, a rhythm that seemed to echo her own heartbeat, and the petals that drifted from the tree glowed brighter with every breath she took.

This was it—the place where the forest's magic began, where every stream, every breeze, and every creature in the Hollow drew its life. Ivy could feel it curling around her, inviting her to become part of it, as though the forest itself were a living story, and she a word waiting to be written.

Brindle the Fox stood just beyond the roots, watching her with quiet reverence. Tansy and Thistle fluttered in the air above her, their wings sparkling like glass in the moonlight. They knew this was a sacred moment—one that would shape the forest's future.

Ivy lifted the staff in both hands, the pendant at its crown gleaming with soft silver light. She could feel the forest's magic thrumming through the wood, eager to be bound, waiting for her to speak the words that would tie her heart to the Hollow forever.

The spell her grandmother had left—written in careful, looping script—unfolded within her mind like the petals of a flower, and Ivy began to recite it aloud, her voice low and steady:

"By the roots that anchor and the branches that rise,

By the breath of wind and the song of skies,

By the water that flows and the earth that remains, I bind my heart to this forest's veins."

The magic surged, warm and fierce, swirling around her in spirals of starlight. The staff hummed in her hands, and the pendant glowed brighter, casting soft beams through the clearing. Ivy could feel the forest wrapping itself around her, not like chains, but like a second skin—a presence that would always be with her, no matter where she went.

"Not as prisoner, nor bound by stone,

But as guardian, wherever I roam.

What breathes in the forest shall breathe in me,

And through me, its magic shall walk free."

The last word left her lips like the final note of a song, and in that moment, the magic unfurled. It rushed through her like a river, flooding her senses with every scent, sound, and sensation the Hollow held: the cool kiss of morning mist, the bright sting of autumn wind, the hum of roots stretching deep into the soil. Ivy gasped, overwhelmed, but she did not falter.

The pendant at the top of the staff shimmered with radiant light, and the great tree at the heart of the Hollow answered in kind—its blossoms glowing brighter, its branches swaying gently in approval. The forest had accepted her, not as a prisoner to be bound within its borders, but as a **guardian who would carry its magic beyond the Hollow's edge.**

The ritual was complete.

The glow of magic settled, dimming to a soft, steady pulse beneath Ivy's skin. She lowered the staff, feeling the warmth of the magic linger in her bones, a quiet presence that whispered promises of strength and guidance.

Tansy and Thistle let out soft, breathless cheers, their wings buzzing with excitement. "You did it!" Thistle cried, spinning in delighted circles. "You really did it!" Tansy's eyes sparkled with pride. "You're the new guardian now, Ivy. The forest is yours."

Brindle padded forward, his amber eyes gleaming. "Not just hers," he murmured, a smile curling at the edges of his mouth. "The Hollow belongs to all who care for it—she's just the one who will carry the magic forward."

Ivy smiled, her heart swelling with quiet joy. She knew now that she wasn't alone—not truly. The magic of the Hollow lived in every stream, every flower, and every whisper of the wind. And it lived within her, too.

As the night deepened, the forest seemed to hum with quiet contentment, the leaves rustling like a lullaby. Ivy rested her hand against the bark of the great tree, feeling its steady pulse beneath her palm.

"You'll never really leave, will you?" she whispered to the forest. The wind stirred in answer, brushing her cheek like a soft, invisible hand. **The Hollow would always be with her.** In every place she went, in every choice she made, the magic would follow.

And that was enough.

A New Path, a Quiet Magic

The sun rose slowly over Windspindle Hollow, the first rays of morning spilling golden light through the trees. Dew sparkled on leaves and petals, and the forest, so recently thrumming with ancient magic, now stretched into the soft quiet of dawn. The path back toward the village lay open, bathed in warm sunlight, as if the Hollow knew that this part of Ivy's journey had reached its end.

Ivy stood at the edge of the heart-tree's clearing, her hand resting lightly on the staff she now carried, the silver pendant nestled in its crown still glowing faintly, as if to remind her: *You are never alone.*

Tansy and Thistle hovered nearby, their usual mischief replaced with solemn understanding. "So... this is goodbye, then?" Thistle asked, his wings slowing to a soft flutter. Ivy smiled warmly at the tiny fairy, a bittersweet ache settling in her heart. "Not goodbye," she said softly. "Just... see you soon."

"You'll come back?" Tansy's voice was hopeful but hesitant, as though daring to believe it.

Ivy knelt and held out a hand, and both fairies flitted down to land gently on her palm. "Of course I will," she whispered. "This place is part of me now. I couldn't leave it behind if I tried."

The fairies buzzed happily, their tiny wings glowing like morning stars. Brindle the Fox padded up to Ivy's side, tilting his head in that sly, knowing way of his. "You humans and your goodbyes," he said with a soft chuckle. "The forest doesn't bother with such things. It simply waits. And when you return, it will welcome you—just as it did before."

Ivy scratched Brindle behind the ears, and the fox closed his amber eyes in quiet contentment. "Thank you," she whispered. "For everything."

Brindle gave a small huff, clearly amused but pleased. "I do love a happy ending," he said with a grin. "Now go on, little guardian. The world is waiting."

The path to **Greenwick** was bathed in morning light, and with every step Ivy took, the forest felt both closer and farther away—like the memory of a song that stays with you long after the melody fades. She didn't need to look back to know that the Hollow would always be there, waiting patiently beneath its canopy of leaves and stars.

The magic within her thrummed softly, settling into a quiet presence that felt more like a companion than a burden. It wasn't loud or overwhelming—it was simply part of her now, woven into her thoughts and her breath, like roots buried deep within the soil of her soul.

As Ivy crossed the **edge of the Hollow** and stepped back onto the familiar cobblestone streets of Greenwick, she felt no fear, no regret. She had made her choice—not to abandon the magic or bind herself to it entirely, but to carry it forward into the world beyond. The forest lived within her now, and through her, it would grow wherever she went.

The village was waking slowly, the air filled with the scent of bread baking and woodsmoke curling from chimneys. Ivy's boots tapped softly against the stone as she made her way through the streets, passing neighbors who glanced at her with curious eyes.

They couldn't see the magic she carried—not fully—but they felt it. It was in the way she moved, in the calm that followed her footsteps, in the kindness that lingered in her gaze like sunlight on water. People smiled as she passed, as if without knowing why.

A familiar voice called out from the bakery door. "Ivy? Is that really you?" Ivy turned to see **Mrs. Alden**, the village baker, wiping her flour-dusted hands on her apron. Her face lit up with surprise and warmth. "Well, if it isn't Liora's granddaughter!" she exclaimed. "It's good to see you, child. You've been gone a while, haven't you?"

Ivy smiled softly. "Not as long as it feels," she replied, her voice gentle as a breeze. Mrs. Alden peered at her closely, a curious glimmer in her eye. "You've changed, haven't you?" she said, though there was no judgment in her tone—only quiet wonder. "There's something about you now... something peaceful."

Ivy tilted her head, considering the words. "I suppose I found something I didn't know I was missing," she said, more to herself than to Mrs. Alden.

The baker gave a knowing nod and handed Ivy a warm roll, the scent of honey and cinnamon rising from the bread. "Well, whatever it is, it suits you," she said kindly. "Welcome home, Ivy."

Later that day, Ivy returned to her grandmother's **cottage**, nestled at the edge of the village where the trees leaned in close, their branches swaying gently as if to greet her. She stood at the gate for a moment, taking in the sight of the house that held so many memories, before stepping through the door.

Inside, everything was just as she had left it—the scent of dried herbs lingering in the air, the little trinkets her grandmother had collected still resting on their shelves. Ivy placed the staff carefully by the hearth, knowing it would wait for her when she needed it.

She took a deep breath, letting the quiet magic within her settle. **The forest was here, too—in the warmth of the wood, in the jars of herbs, in the light that poured through the windows.** Magic, she realized, wasn't confined to a place. It lived in the way you saw the world, in the choices you made, in the love you carried with you. And Ivy knew that she would carry it with her always.

That evening, as the sun dipped low and the sky blushed with the colors of twilight, Ivy sat on the porch with a steaming cup of tea cradled in her hands. The air was cool and sweet, the first stars beginning to blink awake in the deepening sky.

A soft breeze stirred the leaves, and Ivy smiled, feeling the familiar hum of the Hollow's magic in the air. **The forest had not left her. It never would.**

Somewhere in the distance, she heard the faint call of an owl, a sound that reminded her of Brindle's sly grin and the fairies' playful laughter. She knew she would return to Windspindle Hollow one day—but for now, the forest was content to live quietly within her, just as she was content to live with its magic nestled in her heart.

And in that moment, with the night settling gently over the world and the wind whispering promises through the trees, Ivy knew that her journey was only just beginning.

The magic of Windspindle Hollow would follow her, wherever she went.

Epilogue: A Whisper on the Wind

The seasons turned, as they always do. Ivy's life unfolded in small, beautiful moments—conversations over cups of tea, the planting of a garden that grew wild and free, and the quiet joy of knowing she carried something rare and wonderful within her.

Sometimes, when the wind stirred just right, Ivy would pause and listen, a smile curving her lips. **The forest was always there, just beyond the edge of sight, waiting patiently for her next visit.**

And whenever she returned—whether in dreams or in waking hours—Windspindle Hollow would welcome her back, as it always had.

For magic, Ivy had learned, was not in staying or leaving. **It was in the in-between spaces, the places where love and memory meet.**

And that was the truest magic of all.

The End.

"The Heart of Windspindle Hollow"

Beneath the trees where moonlight spills,
And shadows hum through moss-clad hills,
A whispered song drifts soft and low—
The ancient pulse of roots that grow.
The forest breathes, it sighs, it waits,
Through shifting winds and tangled fates.
A fox with amber eyes draws near,
With riddles wrapped in autumn's cheer.
Fairies flit on wings of glass,
Through streams that sing and clouds that pass,
While branches stretch like arms that know
The joy of holding, letting go.
And at the heart, where starlight gleams,
Where rivers speak in silvered dreams,
A girl steps light, both bold and small—
The forest stirs—it knows her call.
She carries loss, she carries love,
And magic hums below, above.
The staff she holds is not a cage,
But ink to write upon life's page.
Not bound by walls, nor kept by key,
Her heart is wild and running free.
For magic isn't held—it flows,
In every path the wanderer goes.
And through her hands, the Hollow blooms,

B. HUMPHREY

In fireflies and fern-fringed rooms.
She'll walk the world with forest's grace,
With starry roots no time can trace.
For what's within will never fade—
A spell in every choice she's made.
She'll carry winds and whisper rain,
And when she leaves, the trees remain.
So listen close when breezes sigh,
Or petals drift beneath the sky—
The magic's there, though worlds may part,
It lives in every open heart.